To Kevin + Cathy —

Toucha

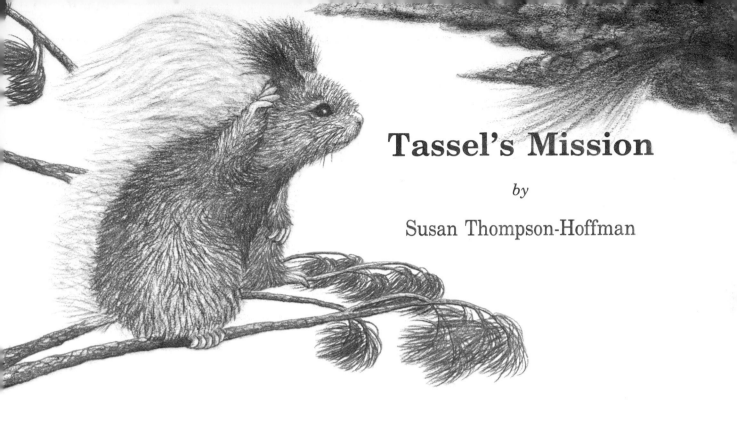

Tassel's Mission

by

Susan Thompson-Hoffman

Like a father calling for his lost child, the wind whistled across the Kaibab Plateau. A fierce storm followed on the heels of the wind. Tassel the Kaibab squirrel fought her way out to the end of a branch that reached far over the Grand Canyon. Lightning struck deep in the rocks and thunder bounced off the canyon walls. Her heart quickened as she rode the branch up and down in the wind.

Many times before, Tassel had climbed out on this branch. Many times before, it had seemed that the wind was about to speak to her.

The wind howled and moaned as it circled Tassel's tree. Once again, Tassel strained to make sense of the sounds, as they wove in and out of the branches. And then, unmistakably, she heard a beautiful sound. The wind called her name.

"Tassel," it said clearly. "Hear me well. For I have a story to tell you. It will be told only once."

Tassel's eyes grew bright with excitement. "A story from the wind!" she whispered in awe. And she leaned far out to hear every word.

"Long ago," the wind sang, "Your ancestors all lived on the south rim of the canyon. During that time, the great bed of the great Colorado River was sometimes dry. One day, a young squirrel left the south rim. She climbed down the canyon wall until she reached the river bed. It was dry, so she darted across. Then she followed a stream bed on this side of the river. Finally, she reached this rim—the north rim. And here she began to raise your side of the family."

Green lightning crackled and thunder rumbled nearby as the wind continued the story.

"No squirrels were ever able to cross the river again. The canyon became deeper with each passing year and the river ran fast and full. One family of squirrels remained on the south rim. They are called the Abert squirrels. But a new family—yours, Tassel—thrived and grew on the north rim. These are the Kaibab squirrels. As time went on, the Aberts became known for their dark tails and light bellies. And the Kaibabs were recognized by their white tails and dark bellies, like yours, Tassel."

Tassel perked up her ears to hear the wind better.

"A family, once whole, is now divided," sighed the wind, as it moved down the canyon. "But there is a way for you to find your family." Tassel struggled to hear. "Find your family," the wind whispered. "Find your family. . . . ."

And then, there was nothing. The wind was gone. Only the distant thunder could be heard. Even the trees were still.

Tassel, too, was still. She repeated the words of the wind in her mind. "It is up to me to find the rest of my family!" she decided.

Suddenly she heard a rustling by her nest below. She looked down. "Prickles," she scolded good-naturedly, "Get away from my nest. Every time you get near it, you leave a mess. One day you will leave a quill behind and I will get stuck with it."

"Oh Tassel, the wind woke me up," said Prickles. "I feel scared. I would give anything for a hug."

Tassel had a special fondness for Prickles. But Tassel did not want to hug a porcupine, even if it were Prickles. She scampered down to Prickles' side. "Oh Prickles, your quills are much too sharp," she laughed gently. "Give yourself a hug and pretend it is from me."

Then she had an idea. "Prickles," she said. "I am going on a long journey. And while I am gone, I am going to ask you to be the keeper of my nest. Guard it carefully. Keep it safe from storms. And, for goodness sake, if you lose any quills, sweep them away from the nest."

When Prickles heard Tassel's news, she began to worry. "Where are you going?" Prickles asked. "Will you come back?"

"Of course I will come back, Prickles. And don't be afraid," replied Tassel softly. "The deer mice will squeal and comfort you. The ravens will caw. And if you listen quietly on a windless day, the canyon wren will sing its sweetest songs for you. But I MUST go. The wind has spoken."

"But where, Tassel?" asked Prickles.

"Over there," said Tassel, pointing toward the south rim. The afternoon light played among the orange and red rocks of the canyon wall.

To prepare for the journey, Tassel pulled apart several pinecones, eating the seeds inside. And then she was off. As her back feet left the soft pine needle floor of the plateau, her whole body shivered. "Whatever am I doing?" she wondered. "Will I be safe from the coyote? Will I find food and a dry place to sleep?" For a moment, she was tempted to return. Then, "No," she whispered firmly. "A decision is a decision, and I have made mine." So she stepped down onto the stone ledges of the canyon wall.

Gravel rolled under her feet as if it were alive. More than once, Tassel had to dig in her claws, while her back legs dangled dangerously from a ledge. Dust blew into her face. Carefully, she picked her way down the steep trail.

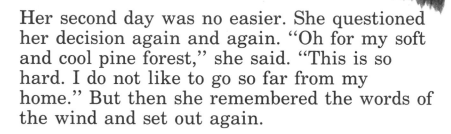

As the last golden light left the sky, Tassel spotted a group of ponderosa pines growing along Bright Angel Creek. She edged along a shelf and leaped into the branches of a tree, like a child into its mother's arms. She curled up against a limb and fell fast asleep.

Her second day was no easier. She questioned her decision again and again. "Oh for my soft and cool pine forest," she said. "This is so hard. I do not like to go so far from my home." But then she remembered the words of the wind and set out again.

Food became more difficult to find. There were fewer trees, and they were farther apart. Often, she slipped in the pebbles and dust, catching herself by her sharp claws just in time. The canyon grew hotter with each step.

And then the wind came once more. It whipped through the canyon, whining and howling. Tassel hoped to hear a message, but no words came. Tassel covered her eyes as the wind tore past. "Speak to me again," she pleaded. "Please." But the wind said nothing.

On the fourth day, Tassel did not think she could go on. She was hanging from a large red rock, searching with her paws for a foothold below. She was tired, and she had eaten little over the last few days. Instead of helping her on her way, the wind had brought dust storms, rain, and gusts to loosen her hold.

Suddenly a raven cawed loudly just above her head. Without thinking, Tassel turned to look. She lost her hold on the large red rock, and fell down the wall of the canyon like a stone.

For a long time, Tassel lay in the dirt, stunned. But slowly the rocks of the canyon came into focus. She got up and brushed the dust and sand from her fur. Then she realized she was not alone. Sleeping under a rock overhang nearby was a ringtail. He lay on his back, because the sun was hot. Just then the ringtail opened his eyes.

"I beg your pardon," said Tassel. "I know this is your time for sleeping. I did not want to wake you up."

"Who are you?" he asked.

"I am Tassel, a Kaibab squirrel," said Tassel.

"A squirrel," said the ringtail to himself. "I'm not above eating a squirrel. But I'm not hungry enough for such a large squirrel. I'll listen to her story."

"I am on a mission to find my family," Tassel continued. "But who are you?"

"The coyote calls me 'Orphan'," the ringtail said. "I have no family. But that won't be so for long, because I am looking for a mate."

"Then we are both looking for a family," said Tassel. "I am on my way to find my cousins who live on the south rim. But I have been traveling for days and am very hungry. Can you help me find some food?"

Orphan pointed to several pinecones that had fallen from a tree high above. Tassel ripped them apart and ate every seed.

"If you are going to the south rim, how will you get across the great river?" asked Orphan. Below, the Colorado River twisted through the rocks like a great pale red snake fleeing from an eagle.

"I haven't exactly worked that part out yet," said Tassel. "Do you have any ideas?"

"No, but you might ask advice from Delver the beaver if you reach the riverbank," said Orphan helpfully. "Delver is very wise."

Tassel thanked Orphan, who pointed out the easiest trail through the trees that lined Bright Angel Creek. She set out on her journey feeling fresh and hopeful. It was a long way to the bottom of the canyon, but she was clearly making progress.

As she leaped from the branches of one cottonwood tree to another along the creek, the sun rose in the sky. The lower walls of the canyon became a furnace. Tassel had left her main food source, the pines, far behind her. By midday, she was thirsty and hungry. Then the sky grew dark. The wind began to moan.

"Perhaps now the wind will speak to me," she said wistfully. But only driving rain followed. "At least it is not so hot," sighed Tassel with a small shiver. She curled up under an overhang, for there were no trees nearby, and fell into a restless sleep.

When she awoke, the sun was beating down again. Tassel had never known such heat. She was used to eating constantly, but she had not seen any food for some time now. Her feet were bleeding and she was thin and ragged. Then, in the distance, she heard the roar of water. She began to run.

She dodged a scorpion basking in the sun. But when a collared lizard darted in front of her, she jumped to one side. She lost her footing, stepping off into thin air. She dropped, end over end, rolling and tumbling down the last of the trail. With a thump, she landed on the river bank.

Dazed, she lay in the sand. Then, "Slap!" A beaver's tail splashed water into her face. She wiped her eyes and looked up.

"Delver?" asked Tassel, hopefully.

"Delver," the beaver confirmed.

"You don't know how glad I am to see you," said Tassel. "I am Tassel, the Kaibab squirrel."

"And so you are!" said Delver, with a twinkle. "From your entrance, I thought you were a flying squirrel!"

"I wish I were," said Tassel, laughing. "I would have gotten down here a lot faster."

"In fact, I am on a mission. The wind came to me and told me to find my family." She pointed up at the south rim. "They live up there," she said. She described her cousins, the Abert squirrels. Then she told him how he could help her. "You could take me across the river, Delver," said Tassel.

Delver looked out at the swift river. "Tassel," said Delver, "I am sorry. But this river is fast and dangerous. While you are thin, you are a large squirrel. The river might sweep us both away if I tried to carry you on my back."

"But I MUST go," said Tassel. "I had hoped that you would come with me up the south wall."

Delver began to laugh. "Tassel, look at me," he said. "I am big. I am fat. I waddle. I am covered with thick hair. My back feet are webbed. Am I suited to climb along rock ledges in the burning heat of the sun? No, Tassel, the river is my home. I cannot leave my river. Not ever."

"But how will I cross the river?" Tassel asked.

Delver sighed. "Tassel, you cannot cross," he said gently. "No squirrel will ever cross this river again. Now the water is high throughout the year. You cannot go over to find your cousins. And they cannot cross to see you. What you have done is astonishing! Remember that. But you can go no farther."

She had been so sure that the wind would help her find a way. All the days of little food, restless sleep, and loneliness, caught up with Tassel. She stared at the river in despair.

Then, one by one, Delver's children came up out of the river. Delver spoke softly to her. "Listen, Tassel. You are thin. You are tired. You need your strength to return home. Try to remember the words of the wind. Could they have a different meaning?"

Tassel looked up at Delver. "Remember, Tassel," Delver went on, "in your blood you already carry a little of the Kaibabs and a little of the Aberts. Their blood was your blood, and your blood was theirs. Your family is not across the canyon. Your family is within you! Go home, Tassel. Go home. You can find your family by raising a tree full of babies. And when you look at your children, see in their tufted ears the Aberts, because the Aberts are there. And in their snowy white tails, the Kaibabs, because the Kaibabs are there too."

Tassel looked at Delver with amazement. Delver had understood the call of the wind. She walked over and put her nose to Delver's in thanks.

Two of Delver's children brought juniper branches to Tassel. They were thick with berries and Tassel ate her fill. Then with a flick of her tail, she turned to head back up the creek bed. "I will never forget all of you," she said. The young beaver kits watched, as she disappeared around a bend.

As she began to climb the rocky canyon walls, a wind rose. It whirled around her and pushed her upward, cooling and lifting her.

Before long, the bright eyes of Tassel's children would sparkle in
the branches of the ponderosa pine like stars in the night sky.
And one day, they too would hear the call of the wind, beckoning
them to find their family.

To my husband, David

The author gratefully acknowledges the technical assistance of naturalists Robert B. Spicer and David Brown of Phoenix, Arizona, and George Ruffner of Prescott, Arizona, Dr. Charles Handley of The Smithsonian Institution, and of her editor, Randy Houk.

Points of Interest in This Book

Text copyright © 1989 by Soundprints Corporation and The Smithsonian Institution. Illustrations copyright © 1989 by Soundprints Corporation, a subsidiary of Trudy Corporation, 165 Water Street, Norwalk, CT 06856. Manufactured by Horowitz/Rae Book Manufacturers, Inc. Designed by Judy Oliver, Oliver and Lake Design Associates. First edition 10 9 8 7 6 5 4 3 2 1.

Library of Congress Cataloging-in-Publications Data
Thompson-Hoffman, Susan   Tassel's Mission
Summary: A tassel-eared squirrel embarks on a perilous mission down the Bright Angel Creek of the Grand Canyon to 'find her family'.
1.   Squirrels—juvenile literature   [1. Squirrels]
1.   Thompson-Hoffman, Susan.   11. Title.
ISBN: 0-924483-00-8